© 2022 Sunbird Books, an imprint of Phoenix International Publications, Inc.
8501 West Higgins Road   34 Seymour Street   Heimhuder Straße 81
Chicago, Illinois 60631   London W1H 7JE   20148 Hamburg

www.sunbirdkidsbooks.com

Library of Congress Control Number: 2021944198

ISBN: 978-1-5037-5712-7 Printed in China

THE BEAR WHO DIDN'T DARE

Written by Susan Rich Brooke
Illustrated by Jenny Palmer

sunbird books

Deep in the woods,
the birds started to sing,
and that's how the little bears
knew it was spring.

The bears ran outside
for the sun and fresh air...

...except Ursa, the littlest.
She **DIDN'T DARE**!
"It's OK," said her mom,
with a smile on her face.
"You'll go when you're ready.
It isn't a race."

As her brothers and sisters
began to explore,
Ursa looked and listened
from her cozy den door.
She saw a butterfly flutter.
She heard a bird tweet.
She caught the scent of a flower.
It smelled so sweet!

Ursa stepped outside
for a closer look.
There was more to explore
with each step she took.

She smelled every violet.
She waved to a wren.
And before she knew it...

...she was **FAR** from the den!

"Let's swim across the lake!" shouted one little bear. But the lake looked so wide, Ursa **DIDN'T DARE**!

"It's OK," said a tortoise,
his voice slow and steady.
"You'll swim the lake
when you're good and ready."

Ursa sat on the shore
and looked at the sky.
The fluffy white clouds
that were drifting by
were shaped like a fish,
a duck, and an otter.
And all the while,
the sun grew hotter.

The water looked cool,
Ursa could see.
She dipped in a paw,
then two, then three.
She paddled a little,
then paddled some more.
And before she knew it...

...she was **FAR** from the shore!

"Let's climb up the tree!"
shouted one little bear.
But the tree looked so tall,
Ursa **DIDN'T DARE**!
"It's OK," called a snail,
who was inching up high.
"You'll climb the tree
when you're ready to try."

The birds started singing
an evening song,
so Ursa decided
to sing along.
She sang about stars,
shining and winking.
And all the while,
the sun was sinking.

Could she reach the star
shining up in the sky?
Ursa wasn't sure,
but she wanted to try.
She grabbed a branch
that felt safe and sound.
And before she knew it...

...she was **FAR** from the ground!

All summer long,
Ursa took her sweet time.

And the bear who **DIDN'T DARE**...

...could now **RUN**, **SWIM**, and **CLIMB**!